To My Lovely Wife Che

&

Awesome Children

(David Jr., Ethan, Asaiah, Anaya, and Laila)

May God continue to give each of you the
***DESIRE** and **POWER** to do what pleases him!*

I Don't Want To Stop Praising God!

First Printing, 2019

ISBN: 978-1723917271

I do not understand the things I do.
I do not do the good things ***I want to do.***
And I do the bad things I hate to do.
Romans 7:15 (ICB)

Yes, God is working in you
to help you ***want to do*** *what pleases him.*
Then he gives you the ***power*** *to do it.*
Philippians 2:13 (ICB)

Praise the Lord from the earth.
Praise him, you large sea animals and all the oceans.
[8] Praise him, lightning and hail, snow and clouds,
and stormy winds that obey him.
[9] Praise him, mountains and all hills,
fruit trees and all cedar trees.
[10] Praise him, you wild animals and all cattle,
small crawling animals and birds.
[11] Praise him, you kings of the earth and all nations,
princes and all rulers of the earth.
[12] Praise him, you young men and women,
old people and children.

Psalm 148:7-12 (ICB)

Excuse me!
My name is Little Dave.
Do animals praise God?
John 3:16
John 3:16

Hello Little Dave!
In Psalm 148:10, God tells the birds to give him praise. So...
Psalm 148:10

John
3:16
Psalm
148:10
John
3:16

I praise God for my
feet, feet, feet!

So I tweet, tweet, tweet!
And I tweet, tweet, tweet!

Psalm
148:10
John
3:16
John
3:16
John
3:16
John
3:16

That's great!
Can we see if the other animals praise God?
Sure, let's go!

John
3:16

I praise God for my
sleigh, sleigh, sleigh!

So I neigh, neigh, neigh!
And I neigh, neigh, neigh!

I praise God for this
yak, yak, yak!!

So I quack, quack, quack!
And I quack, quack, quack!

psalm 106:1
John 3:16
John 3:16
John 3:16
John 3:16

IsAiAh
43 : 20
John
3:16
John
3:16

I praise God because I'm
cute, cute, cute!

So I hoot, hoot, hoot
And I hoot, hoot, hoot!

I love VEGANS
I AM A VEGAN
John 3:16
John 3:16
John 3:16
John 3:16

I praise God for this
boar, boar, boar!

So I roar, roar, roar!
And I roar, roar, roar!

I praise God for this
shark, shark, shark!

So I bark, bark, bark!
And I bark, bark, bark!

John
3:16
John
3:16
John
3:16

John
3:16
John
3:16

I praise God for my
cloak, cloak, cloak!

So I croak, croak, croak!
And I croak, croak, croak!

And I praise God for this
calf, calf, calf!

So I laugh, laugh, laugh!
And I laugh, laugh, laugh!

Psalm 126:2
John 3:16
John 3:16
John 3:16

John
3:16
John
3:16

So the animals praise God with...

a tweet, tweet, tweet

a neigh, neigh, neigh

a quack, quack, quack

a hoot, hoot, hoot

a roar, roar, roar

a bark, bark, bark

a croak, croak, croak

and a laugh, laugh, laugh!

That's great!

HOSPITAL BILL
WATER
PAST DUE
NOTICE OF DISCONNECTION BILL
HEALTH REPORT
John 3:16
John 3:16

But why isn't Mr. Jones praising God? And what happened to the colors?
The colors will return if he praises God.
We need to help him!

John 3:16
John 3:16
John 3:16
John 3:16

I want the colors to return but I can't think of any reasons to praise God.

Please help me Little Dave!

Don't worry Mr. Jones.

I can help you! There are many reasons to praise God!

Caring
Funny
Faithful
Friendly
Cool
Awesome
Alive Cool
Everlasting
Excellent Forgiving Eternal
Big and Strong
Fun Eternal Forgiving Honest
Good
Everlasting
Holy
Amazing
Amazing
Holy
Awesome
Good
Alive
Friendly
Caring
Fun
Funny
Honest
Faithful
Excellent

We should praise
God because He is...

Neat
Wise
Pure
Real
Lord
True
Powerful Perfect Jesus • Just
Kind and Loving
The Best Powerful Honest Honest
Patient
PERFECT
Mighty
Loyal
Super
Pure
Wise
Real Neat
The Best
Super
Patient
King
Loyal
True Mighty
Jesus
Nice Nice

I praise God as my King, King, King!

So I sing, sing, sing...

And I sing, sing, sing...
And I sing, sing, sing!
John 3:16
John 3:16
John 3:16
John 3:16

The colors are back!
Thank you God! I don't want to stop praising you!
John 3:16
John 3:16

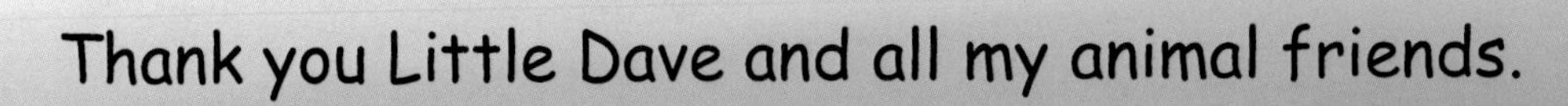
Thank you Little Dave and all my animal friends.

Psalm
148:10
PSALM
126:2
John
3:16

Now, let's praise God together!

Check out our cool **John 3:16 shoes**. We use the colored stripes on our shoes to share the love of God with others.

John 3:16 says that God loved the world so much that he gave his only Son **Jesus**. God gave his Son so that whoever believes in him may not be lost, but have eternal life.

Read the next page to learn the meaning of each color.

GOLD reminds us of a perfect God who created everything. God wants us to live forever with him in a place called heaven because HE loves us.

Genesis 1; Revelation 21:18-27

BLUE reminds us of a problem that we have called sin. That big word means doing things God doesn't want us to do; things like being mean to people and not sharing our toys. By the way everyone sins, even your parents. God hates sin! He will not allow us into heaven because of our sins. ***Isaiah 59:2; Romans 3:23 & 6:23***

RED reminds us of Jesus Christ. He is the only one who can solve our problem. Someone had to pay for all the bad things that we do. Jesus came to earth to take the punishment for our sins by dying on the cross and rising again on the third day. ***John 3:16 & I Corinthians 15***

WHITE reminds us that we can be made clean by asking God to forgive us for our sins. We also have to admit that Jesus Christ is Lord and believe that he rose from the grave to pay for our sins.

Romans 10:9-10

GREEN reminds us of life. We will live forever with God in heaven, but God wants us to enjoy him now by praying, reading the bible, giving, going to church, serving, and sharing this good news with others.

II Peter 3:18

Check out what the Bible has to say about praising God! Pick one verse and review it for the entire month. Do this for all 12 months. Ask your parents or friends to join you in memorizing the verses.

12 Verses in 12 Months

January

Every wild and tame animal, all reptiles and birds, come praise the LORD!
Psalm 148:10 (CEV)

February

Praise the Lord!
Thank the Lord because he is good. His love continues forever.
Psalm 106:1 (ICB)

March

Even the wild animals will be thankful to me. The wild dogs and owls will honor me.
Isaiah 43:20A (ICB)

April

Then we were filled with laughter, and we sang happy songs.
Then the other nations said, "The Lord has done great things for them." **Psalm 126:2 (ICB)**

May

But we will praise the Lord now and forever. Praise the Lord!
Psalm 115:18 (ICB)

June

Let everything that has breath praise the LORD. Praise the LORD!
Psalm 150:6 (ICB)

Check out what the Bible has to say about praising God! Pick one verse and review it for the entire month. Do this for all 12 months. Ask your parents or friends to join you in memorizing the verses.

12 Verses in 12 Months

July

Praise him, you kings of the earth and all nations, princes and all rulers of the earh.

Psalm 148:11(ICB)

August

Let them praise the Lord
Because they were created by his command.

Psalm 148:5 (ICB)

September

Praise him, you young men and women, old people and children.

Psalm 148:12 (ICB)

October

Praise the Lord from the earth.
Praise him, you large sea animals,and all the oceans.

Psalm 148:7 (ICB)

November

Praise HIM for his strength.
Praise HIM for his power.

Psalm 150:2 (ICB)

December

Praise the Lord.
He alone is great.
He is greater than heaven and earth. **Psalm 148:13 ICB**

About the Author

David Jean-Julien created the **"I Don't Want To"** book series to help children discover the heart of God.

David is a professor, counselor, and lover of God's Word. He received his master's degree from Trinity International University in Deerfield, Illinois. David and his wife Chebby live in the Washington, D.C. area with their five children.

Check out our "I Don't Want To" books:

Made in the USA
Middletown, DE
26 August 2023